On a distant island lived a wolf.
A wolf who was clever. The greatest
inventor in all the wide world.

She had machines to
wash her fur . . .

make her
bed . . .

THE WONDER MACHINE

BARRY TIMMS

LAURA BRENLLA

LITTLE TIGER
LONDON

and pick apples from her orchard.
But Wolf wanted more.
"I will make a machine to
change the world for ever!"
she declared.

Then in her workshop
Wolf found a book.
A book with no name.

And inside it she read:

Wolf's eyes widened. "That's it!" she gasped.

Wolf set to work at once. But there were three things she just could not find:

a fishing reel,

a garden rake

and a slotted silver spoon.

"Bother!" Wolf huffed and stomped outside. She paused at the spot where she did her best thinking.

"Perhaps I'll sail to the village,"
she said, looking out across
the water. She had never left
home before.

. . . Wolf worked wonders!
  "I can't thank you enough!"
said a squirrel, rushing over
with some cool orangeade.

Then Wolf told Squirrel her plan:

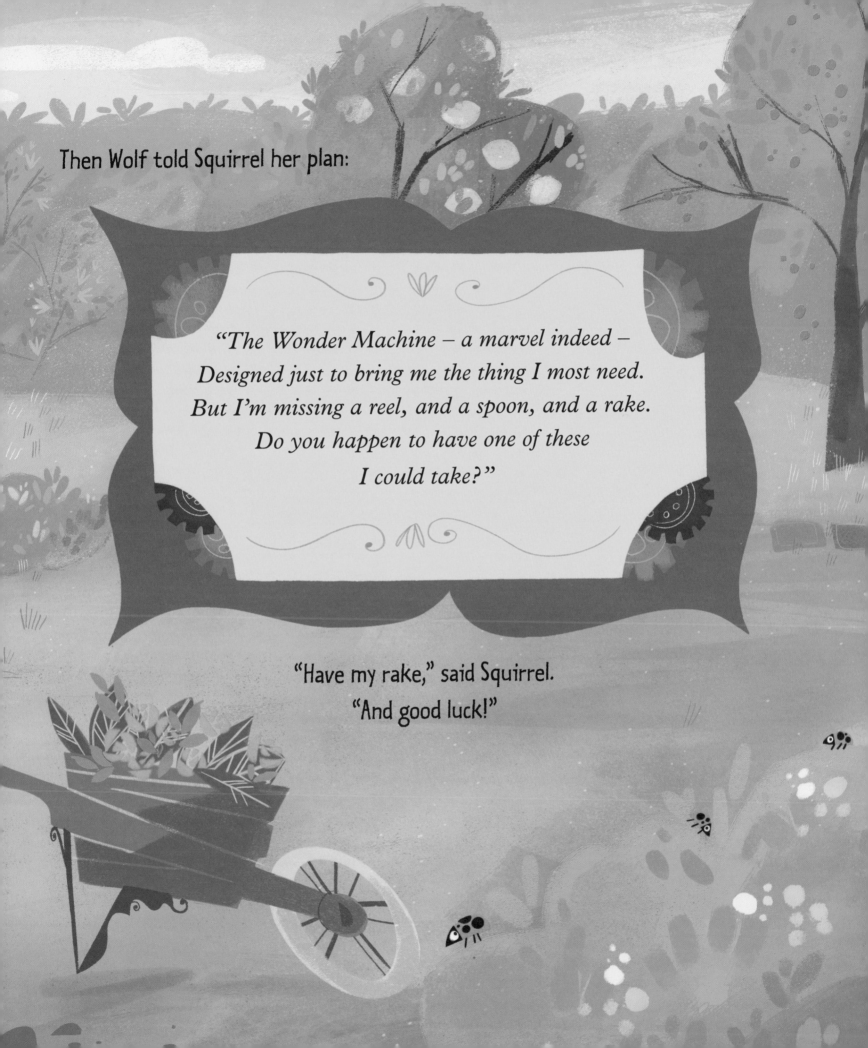

"The Wonder Machine – a marvel indeed –
Designed just to bring me the thing I most need.
But I'm missing a reel, and a spoon, and a rake.
Do you happen to have one of these
I could take?"

"Have my rake," said Squirrel.
"And good luck!"

Next Wolf met an owl. "Is that your boat?" she asked.
"Yes," said Owl, "but it's too battered to sail."
Wolf's eyes twinkled. "Come help me," she said.

So together they turned the boat over.

And with a tip and a tap, the two worked wonders!

Then Wolf told Owl of her plan and the things she still needed.
"Take this fishing reel," said Owl. "And thank you!"

News travelled fast in the village.

"It's the wolf who works wonders!"
cried two fox cubs. "Can you fix our toys?"

And with a tip and a tap, Wolf did just that.

"How kind you are," said the father fox. "And Squirrel told me all about your plan:

The Wonder Machine – it's the talk of the town! It makes a bright smile out of every frown!"

Fox had a surprise for Wolf.

"I hear you need a silver spoon," he said. "Please take this one in return. And do stay for dinner."

Wolf sailed home in the moonlight.
She slept well, then tipped and tapped
all day till at last her machine was ready.

"The wonders this will bring!" said Wolf,
her tail twitching.

She turned the machine's handle.
Cogs clattered.
Pistons pumped.

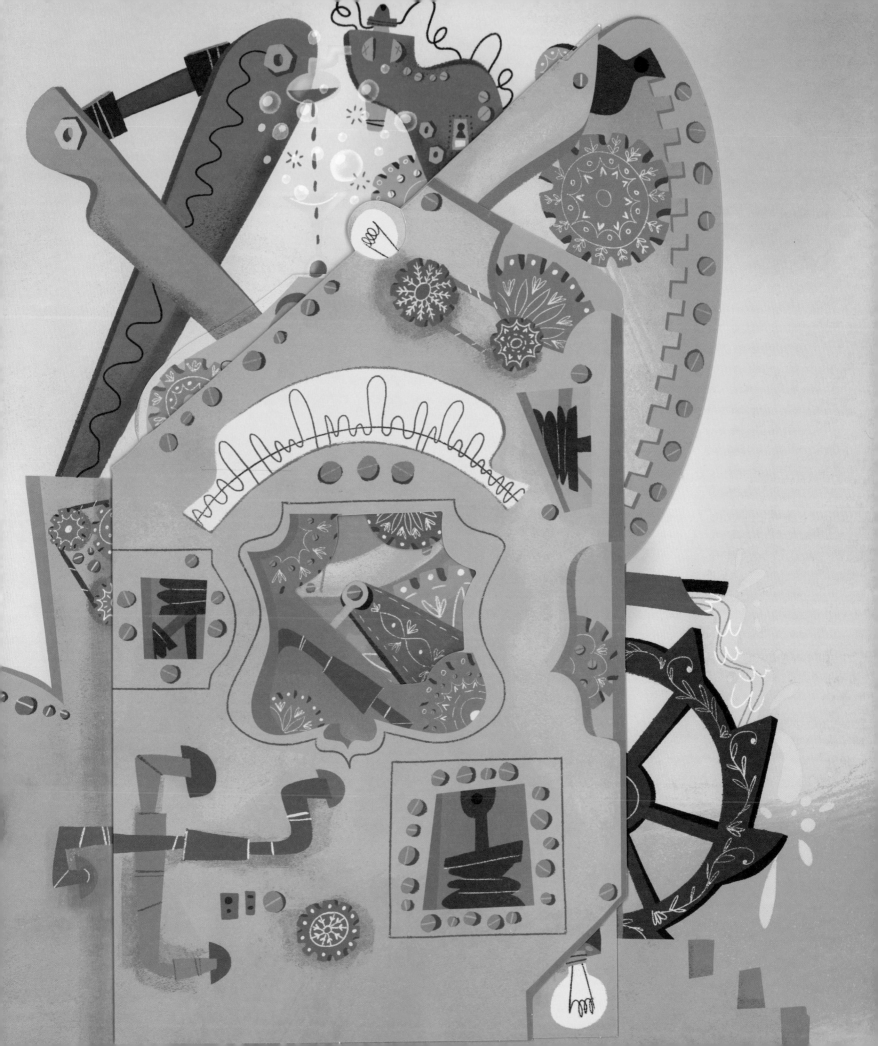

But when the music ended,
Wolf slumped sadly. She felt
empty, and rather alone.

She thought of the villagers,
of their songs and dancing.
"The machine has got it
wrong!" Wolf howled. "I don't
need music, I need friends!"

Then a sound caught her ear.
"More music?" she whispered.
But the Wonder Machine was silent.
The sound was coming from the shore . . .

It was the animals from the village!
And they were singing this song:

"The Wonder Machine
plays a wonderful tune –
We followed its sound
by the light of the moon,
To say these three cheers for
the wolf who can mend.
How happy we are to
have you as our friend!"